# OPERATION

Kick
BUTT

**Read more about Al's
crazy adventures in:**

Operation Itchy Bum

# OPERATION Kick BUTT

## Niki Daly

Hodder
Children's
Books

A division of Hachette Children's Books

*For Muzzie*
*with love from Niki*

# Chapter One

Have I told you about the time I rescued my mum from making the biggest *ever* mistake in her *entire* life?

See, she was about to marry this psycho teacher – well, ex-teacher now, because he was discovered to be the world's worst liar and cheat – *and* violent on top of it! Tried to strangle me!

He's a TV personality now.

After that, my dad and mum got back together and something *really* amazing happened – Tom was born. Tom-Tom's our genius baby. Swear it! He can draw a map of England using spilt prune yogurt. And when he was, like, eighteen months he started to spell – using letters dug out of his alphabetti-spaghetti. Especially, all the 'o's. First, they made no sense at all – like:

But soon they started to look like real-sounding words:

I'd read them for him and he'd wet himself laughing. He's almost two now and can read. Well, almost. Actually, his idea of a good book is how easy it is to chew off the corners.

Talking about amazing . . . my gran went to Japan and became a Yubiwaza champion. *I swear!* She read about it from an ad in one of my comics. So, off she goes and trains with a guy called Black Dragon. She can now paralyze a 200-kilo attacker with just one finger!

'That's *ridonkulous!*' laughs Sophie, my best friend.

'Not really,' I tell her. 'Yubiwaza requires outstanding balancing skills, and Gran has that – see, she's been wearing mega platform heels since she was twelve, and has never come off them.'

'You like to exaggerate, don't you,' says Sophie, giving me that sly look.

I just act as though I don't know *what* she's on about. I mean, these things happen, you know. And as Mr Maythem, our really nice 6th grade teacher, says:

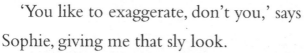

'*Life is stranger than fiction.*'

Take last hols, for instance.

# Chapter Two

'Drop the volume, Androids!' shouts Mr
Maythem.

That's what he calls us – *Androids!* Mr
Maythem thinks humans are really aliens that
got put together in ancient laboratories by space
men who visited earth billions of years ago
from some far distant galaxy.

'Serious, sir?' we ask.

'No, Sirius!' he answers, looking chuffed with
his little joke. 'Also known as the Dog Star in
the constellation Canis Major,' he adds.

Now, we really don't know what to believe. There's no end to Mr Maythem's far-out ideas. He says that pigs are actually holding cells for the souls of *really* greedy people who always go for supersize burgers and fatty chips. He says that's why pigs have eyes like humans. And I think he might be right on this one because I once looked into the eyes of a piggy and I swear I heard this tiny, desperate voice calling out: *'Help! . . . Let me out!'*

As you may guess, Mr Maythem's into conspiracy theories – big time! For instance, he thinks Michael Jackson and his sister, Latoya, were the same person. We tell him that that *can't* be, because Michael is dead and his sister is still alive, see.

'She's a hologram,' he tells us, coolly.

*'No ways!'* we protest. Honestly, sometimes I think he's mental and having us on. But you can't tell with Mr Maythem. He's, like, dead serious when he tells us these things.

Take now –

'In the future, none of you might have work. It will all be left for machines to do. So people are going to have to find other things to occupy themselves with, like – looking after one another.'

We gawp at each other, wondering where this is heading.

'*Community Service!*' he says to us. 'We are all going to have to get involved with work that machines can't do. And that's caring for one another.'

So, *that's* it – our holiday project. We might have guessed.

Mr Maythem makes suggestions:

1. Volunteer for the RSPCA (I like dogs – don't fancy their poo!)

2. Clean up the polluted canal that runs at the bottom of our sports field (been there, done that, and had to throw away the smelly T-shirt)

3. Work in a soup kitchen for the homeless who squat under the northbound flyover (Oooh, don't know about that!)

4. Offer our services around our neighbourhood to any needy folk (yawn!)

'You can work on your own, but for safety's sake I'd much prefer you to work in groups. There're some weirdos out there – shape shifters . . . greys . . . Men in Black . . . tattooed ladies who steal kids for strange acts in weird circuses . . .'

We laugh . . . nervously.

At least I know who I want to team up with – Sophie Ross and Julian Pettifer. See, we're very different – Sophie, Julian and me – but we go together like . . . a . . . a Bombay Pizza. Sophie's like the pickled pineapple – sweet, and sometimes sour! Julian's a nerd, and a bit hard to digest – so he's the curried chicken. I'm Alistair D'arcy McDermott (you can call me Al) and I suppose I must be the extra cheese and garlic because Mum often says, *'Alistair D'arcy McDermott – you're just tooooo much!'*

By the way, you can get Bombay Pizza at Raymoondo Banergee's Curry Cafe on the high street – but more about that later.

# Chapter Three

Later!

Me, Sophie and Julian park our butts on the squeaky plastic seats in Raymoondo's Curry Cafe. If you do a *'slow slide'* you can get a really good fart out of it, which always embarrasses Sophie and makes Julian hide behind the menu – his way of ignoring me!

The reason we're here and not at Macs is because it's a Friday. And on Fridays Raymoondo Banergee, the owner, has a 'Special' on the menu – *Masala Chips, plus* a free glass of Coke and a date ball.

Raymoondo's amazing – on Saturday nights he has Curryoake at his cafe, with fiery hot curry on the menu and karaoke for anyone crazy enough to stand up and belt out some bum-shaking Bollywood hit. Dad had a go once, and I had to crawl under the table and stay there until it was all over!

Raymoondo's also a bit of a mind reader and can always guess what we're going to choose before we do.

'Three Masala Chips, free Cokes and date balls . . . to die for,' he announces, bringing over our order. 'For the lady . . . and the two gents. Enjoy!' We smile at each other and tuck into the yummy, soggy, spiced chips.

'So,' starts Sophie, waving a chip in the air, 'I'm *not* working with animals. I have enough of them at home . . . and that's just my brothers!'

We laugh. Sophie has two teenage brothers who play in a punk rock band called *The Test Icicles*. Get it? Besides not playing in tune they don't wash and always have bits of breakfast dangling from their blue-painted lips. Really *gnarly*!

'So, any ideas?' I propose.

'Well, I've been thinking,' says Julian, who when he thinks, always closes his eyes, drums his fingers and purses his lips as though he's thinking of world events.

'Yes, I've been thinking . . .' he says, 'that there must be some *gaps* in the community service market.'

'Like?' asks Sophie, delicately wiping her mouth with a red and gold paper napkin.

'Well, for instance . . . cleaning old people's spectacles. Have you noticed how many old people walk around shopping malls peering through smeared lenses?'

'Nooooooo!' I say.

'Next!' snaps Sophie.

'Have you noticed how many people let their dogs poop on the street?' I ask, thinking up an idea as I go along while ignoring their blank stares. 'It's against the law!' I explain. 'So, what if we photograph the culprits as they walk off without cleaning after their mutts . . . and . . . and report them if they don't pay up.'

Sophie's unimpressed. Well, I can see my awesome scheme's going nowhere, so I quickly add, 'Then we can give the money to the RSPCA and *that* will be our service to the community. What do you say?'

Sophie looks as though she might choke on a

chip. Julian drains his Coke and lets out a well-controlled burp.

*'I can't believe you!'* splutters Sophie. *'That's blackmail!'*

'I'm afraid it is, Al,' says Julian, backing her up. 'Otherwise, it's a brilliant scheme ... for the criminally insane.'

'Well, I don't fancy another mucky session along that smelly canal,' I mutter. 'Last time I picked up – WITH MY BARE HANDS – what I thought were ... '

'Date balls!' Raymoondo interrupts the flow.

'... well, they were *not* date balls! I'll tell you that!' I say, taking a bite out of mine. I let the sweet taste of dates and coconut drive out all yucky thoughts of picking up waste along the grimy canal.

'This clearly needs a lot more thought,' says Julian, going at his date ball like a squirrel with a nut. 'I suggest we meet tomorrow and . . . give it a lot more thought.' Sophie and I nod in agreement.

'It's so great not to have to think about school on Monday,' sighs Sophie as we step outside.

'Maybe by then we'll know what we'll be doing to serve our fellow man,' says Julian. See? Only a nerd talks like that!

Raymoondo pops his head out and calls after us, 'What about my date balls! Enjoy them?'

'To die for!' Sophie calls back, and we make our way to the crossroads, where Sophie turns left and Julian, right. I carry straight on, taking a short cut home through the park, wondering . . . wondering what I can do to serve my fellow man, as Julian puts it.

*Something that machines can't do!*

As I approach the duck pond, I spot some

rubbish floating around its edge. I pass by, and without giving it much thought, pull out a polystyrene cup and crisp packet and dump them into a bin. Nearby, an old man sitting on a bench sees what I've done and smiles. I smile back. Now, is *that* something machines can ever do?

Make someone smile?

# Chapter Four

*Beep! beep!*

Tom–Tom's standing on a chair pressing the microwave button with his moist little finger.

'Musn't touch, Thomas!' says Mum, moving him away.

'How else is he going to learn about microwaves?' I chip in.

'Micowaaay!' he gurgles as Mum passes him to me. Straight away, the finger goes right up my nose! 'Noooobe!' he tells me (dead keen on pressing buttons and putting his finger into holes is our Tom-Tom). I drop him in his high chair and put some of my old Lego in front of him. Immediately, he builds steps with two pieces, and the rest goes into his slimy mouth. Mum dashes forwards and scoops them out in a flash. They're covered in baby goo.

'*Phwoar!* That's so gross!' I squirm.

'What's so gross?' asks Gran, breezing in.

Now that she's giving art lessons at the Lady Buxom Home for Seniors down the road, Gran visits us quite a lot. I point to the slimy Lego on the table and explain, 'Mum's just rescued that from Tom-Tom's mouth.'

'Oh, that's nothing!' says Gran. 'You should see where my fingers have been. Today, I saved Mr Jeffries from swallowing his dentures, bless him. That was before Mrs Hodges turned herself into abstract art by splattering paint all over the show. Honestly, I spend more time cleaning up than teaching art down there. Mrs Black, that's the new supervisor, thinks it's a waste of time . . .'

Mum pours tea and we sit down, because once Gran starts, she gets on a roll and then it's one story after another. Mum says that's where I get my *motor-mouth* from. Well, I don't mind – Gran's stories are great!

'What I say,' she continues, 'is that old folk need to be stimulated. She's a very odd woman, that Mrs Black. Can't quite put my finger on it, but there's something pretty weird about her.'

We're all ears. Tom–Tom stops banging Mum's phone with his mug and gets this forced, lopsided smile going – which means only one thing.

*'Whoa! Chocolate time!'* I laugh.

Mum gives me that *'don't just sit there laughing'* stare.

'He's your baby!' I chuckle, holding my nose. *Pheuw!*

She picks Tom–Tom up and leaves me and Gran feeling very pleased that *WE* don't have a stinky baby to clean up. When the air's cleared

Gran continues her story about the strange Mrs Black. 'Where was I? Oh yes, as I said – she's rather weird, that woman. I've never seen a face plastered with *soooooo* much makeup. And she has this teensy-weensy, whispery, girly voice but says the most awful things about the residents, like – *"How are my little wrinkly-dinkles doing today?"* I mean, that's no way to talk about old folk, is it? And just the other day, I caught her smoking . . . and *blowing smoke into some old lady's eyes!* Can you *belieeeve* it?'

I do love listening and talking to Gran. She's an artist and *reeeally* cool. She doesn't pull funny faces when I say things like, 'Mr Fenshaw (that's our gym teacher) has got a face like a bag of bums' and things like that. In fact, I've learnt quite a lot of funny expressions from *her*.

'Billowing Bloomers!' she exclaims. 'They're such a funny, sweet old lot.'

And I hear all
about them:
There's Miss Avery,
who Gran says
paints the most
*darling* pink cats
with purple
mascara and
blue-blue eyes.

There's Major
Maddocks who's as
bald as a marble and
barks more than talks,
but a real darling and
war hero, Gran says.

Then her *favourite* old person is someone called
Violet Rose. Gran says she's like a walking
chandelier – with jewels simply *dripping* from her.

And then there's Sailor Flynn –
'His real name is Jim Flynn,
and he has a mermaid
tattooed from his neck
down to his butt,'
Gran explains, with
a wicked smile.

'How do you know?' I chip in.

'Never mind how I know! Tell me about your holiday plans,' she replies, quickly steering the conversation away from tattooed mermaids and Sailor Flynn's butt.

I tell her about the community service project our group are meant to do. But that we haven't made up our minds *what* that will be . . . just yet.

'We can do with some help down at the Lady Buxom,' she says. 'There's always something that needs doing for the old folk – shopping, taking them out in their wheelchairs for a little fresh air. Just listening to them will cheer them up no end.'

I start thinking about it. *Mmmm*, old folk . . . perhaps, they're a bit too much like Tom-Tom – needing to be watched and cleaned up all the time. My face must say it all because Gran gives me a friendly shove from across the table and says, 'Oh, come on! It'll be fun. And you never know – a few of those oldies are pretty well off and have no one to leave their money to. You may just end up inheriting all Violet Rose's fortune!'

*Mmmm* . . . suddenly, I'm interested!

# Chapter Five

Sophie and Julian like the idea.

'It'll be like having lots of grannies and granddads,' says Sophie, sweetly.

'Maybe I could teach them some computer skills,' says Julian.

'Well, Gran says if we're interested, we should go down there this morning and talk to the woman in charge . . . Mrs Black.'

I don't tell them of my secret plan to inherit some old biddy's fortune.

It would be great to hang around the mall all

day since it's the holidays, but this project's got
to get done, so we finish our Cokes and head
off to the old folks' home. When we get there, I
lead the way, following Gran's directions to the
recreation room. On our way, we catch glimpses
of old people sitting in their rooms – some
asleep in their chairs, some leaning as though
they are about to fall over. A few wave to us.

'*Good morning!*' chirps Sophie, so brightly that it makes them smile. And they don't look half as old when they smile.

'Welcome, darlings!' Gran greets as we stroll into the room where she teaches art. Without staring, I get a good look at what's going on. There are quite a few old people sitting at tables wearing smocks. They look a bit like very old

children getting ready for pre-school art. 'We're going to be doing some clay modelling today,' Gran explains.

'These your grandchildren, Beryl?' asks one old biddy, swinging around in her wheelchair. Her mass of jewellery makes a tinkling sound as she stretches out to shake my hand.

This must be Violet Rose.

Gran holds me by the shoulders and introduces us. 'This is Alistair, my grandson, and these are his friends, Sophie and Julian.'

'So, do either of you two want a granny?' asks an old blue-haired lady, looking at Sophie and Julian. She has purple around her eyes and is painting a cat. Sophie giggles and Julian goes red.

After introductions, Gran tells the old biddies that they must carry on with their art while she takes us for our appointment with Mrs Black. I hear one old gent, who looks like a Muppet, clear his throat and grumble, 'Hrrarf, hrrarf . . . let's hope Walkie-Talkie won't keep you the whole morning!'

On our way to the office I ask Gran who 'Walkie-Talkie' is.

'That's the Major's name for Mrs Black, because she's all over the place and never stops talking,' Gran says.

When we get to Mrs Black's office, I'm shocked right out of my socks. The last time I saw a face like that was on a killer clown in a Ghost Tunnel.

Brrrrr! I'm not going to sleep tonight!

I notice that Sophie's not smiling any more and Julian's specs have suddenly misted up. They can't believe their eyes either! You could paint a wall with the amount of make-up Mrs Black has plastered all over her face. It's like looking at a really weird painting by Picasso – with those blood-red lips and greasy mascara eyes with two black slashes for eyebrows.

'Gran tells me that you would like to volunteer your services to the Lady Buxom Home for Seniors,' she says in a tinny voice that sounds as though it's coming from a little girl . . . sitting on a ventriloquist's lap! Only, she's a big girl . . . built like a lumberjack.

I half expect her to topple over and land on me as she teeters forwards in her high heels with their mile-long pointy toes. Suddenly, her hand engulfs mine – like a whale swallowing a pilchard. Her painted nails gleam like vampire fangs at the end of fingers that look strong enough to pull the heads off chickens.

'Y-yes,' I reply. 'We have a community service project for the holidays, and . . .' I seem to have left my body. I'm unable to talk and look at that face at the same time.

'And we'd love to help the old people,' says Sophie, helping me out. The warm touch of Gran's hands on my shoulders brings me back to my senses.

'Yes, and we're w-willing to do a-anything,' I stammer.

'I see,' she says. 'Let me think now . . .' (and she taps a long fingernail on her nut-cracking teeth – tap, tap tap!) 'Ah, yes! The toilets need a good scrubbing . . . and there's always soiled laundry to tackle. These messy old codgers are forever soiling themselves. You'd think they've forgotten where their mouths are . . . not to mention their other parts!'

*What a horrid person!*

My shoulders tense up at the thought of the jobs she wants us to do. I mean, when I said *'anything'* I wasn't exactly thinking of *hard labour*! Quickly, Gran comes to the rescue.

'I thought that Al could help me with my art classes,' she suggests.

Now Sophie looks desperately at Gran for help. 'And I thought Blaire could do with Sophie's help in the hair salon,' is Gran's suggestion.

'So . . . what can we find for this fine, intelligent-looking boy?' asks Mrs Black. Julian starts bobbing up and down nervously as Mrs Black's piercing eyes fall on him.

'I'm rather good at computer science,' he pipes up.

'Ah, a little nerd,' I hear her say under her breath. 'Well, there's bound to be *something* for you to do around here.'

'There is,' says Gran. 'A few people have been given computers by their children and I'm sure Julian can show them how to use the internet and send emails. I hear he's somewhat of a genius.' Julian looks like a man on death row who's just been saved from the electric chair.

'Very well,' says Mrs Black, sourly. 'Now I must see if cook has managed to ration this week's supply of food. She piles far too much on these old people's plates, and they really don't need over-feeding. I mean, sitting around like vegetables doesn't exactly burn up calories, does it? I've said to Blaire, really, why they want their hair done every week is beyond me. It's not like these coffin-dodgers are going anywhere . . . talk about the living dead! Some people just don't know when it's time to leave the party. We put down old pets, so why not . . . '

She seems to have forgotten that we're still in

her office. I look to Gran for a cue. She raises an eyebrow and looks as though she'd be glad to pull the plug – *if* there was one to disconnect Walkie-Talkie! But there's not. Gran points us to the door with a quick nod of the head and we slip out, leaving Mrs Black rattling on like a clogged drain.

Away from the office, Sophie gasps, 'I can't *believe* that! Did you hear what she called the sweet old people?'

'Told you she was strange, didn't I?' says Gran.

'STRANGE!' I say. 'She's *Rocky Horror Picture Show* meets *Nightmare on Elm Street*!'

Afterwards we all have a good laugh, but we're stopped in our tracks when Julian says, 'Actually, I thought she was rather entertaining . . . a very novel way of speaking.' That's Julian for you! Nothing's too weird for him. I suppose

it's all those crazy computer games he plays —
with characters whose brains hang out and
gobble up tins of cat food to score points.

As we approach the recreation room Gran
relaxes. For a while, I thought she might put her
foot in Mrs Black's mean potty-mouth. But it
takes a lot to rattle my gran.

'OK, sweeties — time to start your good
work,' she says. Then she asks one of the staff to
introduce Julian to Mr Broomhall, who's keen
to start emailing his son in Australia. Then she
and Sophie set off to the hair salon, and I'm left
standing outside the recreation room. 'Go in!'
Gran calls over her shoulder. 'They don't bite!'

Not knowing what I'm expected to do, I
slowly open the door . . . and walk nervously
into the room, where the smell of clay and
flowery old ladies hangs in the air.

'Wish my arms were as long as an

octopussy's,' I hear Violet Rose say. She's leaning dangerously forwards in her wheelchair, trying to reach a lump of clay that's lying on the floor under the table. I go over and pick it up for her.

'Bless you, luvvie,' she says, giving me a twinkly smile that makes me feel all funny inside . . . like I've done something amazing, when, really, all I've done is . . . bend down and pick up something for an old lady in a wheelchair.

But it makes me think. It can't be easy being old.

# Chapter Six

*'I'm so old, when I was a kid rainbows were black and white.'*

The oldies are full of jokes. They're not *anything* like Mrs Black makes them out to be. They're quite funny about her too. Especially the Major, who makes sounds like an old dog with a half-hearted bark – I really like him. And Miss Avery and her funny cats. Sailor Flynn's also fun. He whistles all the time, and is rather quick-footed in his trainers for an old geezer.

But the one I like most of all is Violet Rose – Gran's favourite.

Let me describe her for you. She's this little old lady who doesn't seem at *all* old. Like, there's a young girl – Sophie's age – smiling at you from behind the most twinkling blue eyes you've ever seen. And around those eyes are lots of wrinkles, that Gran calls laughter lines. And she talks cockney. Like, 'I'd love a cup of Rosie!' – and that must mean a cup of tea – because Miss Avery turns around and asks, 'You take three spoons don't you, Vi?' And the Major adds, 'No, she takes four. That's what keeps her so sweet – *Huurum! Huurum!*'

This makes Violet Rose giggle and all her jewels go 'tinkle tinkle'.

Well, we're all getting on *really* famously when Mrs Black barges in and says, *'I don't want to have to repeat myself, so turn up those hearing aids!'*

They stare coldly at her.

'We're having to cut back on our little luxuries. So, there'll be no pudding this week,' she informs them. 'And from now on, you'll have to supply your own toilet rolls. Have we all understood? Yes . . . no? Earth to Mars! Would you like it in hieroglyphics?'

They shake their heads . . . in disgust. But when she's gone, they look as though a bomb's just been dropped.

'If things carry on like this, we'll have to take our empty pudding bowls and go begging on the streets,' says one.

'As it is, I can't make ends meet on my pension,' complains another.

Sailor Flynn stops his cheerful whistling and says, 'Tell you wot! Since she took over, this place has gone to the dogs. In fact, Battersea Dogs' Home sounds five star compared to here.'

'Mrumphff!' The Major snorts and says gruffly, *'That woman is as unsettling as a laxative!'* They all find it very funny. But I can see that they're really upset by Mrs Black.

'I haven't had my medicine for the last two months.'

'I hear she plans to increase what we pay around here.'

'And for what! Last week's veg soup had two carrots and a pea floating in some salty water. As appetizing as cat's piddle, I say!'

'The public phone stopped working soon after she arrived. Then she had the cheek to charge us two quid to make a call from her office. Daylight robbery!'

'Night time, too! Left a twenty note by my bedside . . . gone in the morning!'

'Took that fine oil painting of mine to get valued. And I'm still waiting for it to be returned,' huffs the Major, furiously rolling his ball of clay.

The list of complaints grows and work comes to a standstill. Gran has listened to it all and says she'll have a word with Mrs Black.

'Fat lot of good that'll do,' grumbles the Major. 'She thinks we're a lot of old senile fools!' All *he* needs is a cannon for his big ball of clay, and I'm sure he'd declare war on Mrs Black.

Gran asks me to wheel Violet Rose back to her room. It seems to take ages getting there through the maze of corridors. There must be over a hundred old folk living in the Lady Buxom, and each one has their name on their door. Some have pictures from magazines stuck on as well – dogs, flowers, countryside, grandchildren. We pass one with a photo of a nude lady – Sailor Flynn's room!

When we reach the one that says, *'Miss Violet*

*Rose'*, I push her through and park the
wheelchair in the middle of the room. On the
wall there are photos. I go over and look at the
one with three beautiful ladies, posing with
peacock feathers.

'You'd never say it now, but that's me in the
middle,' Violet Rose points out. 'Called
ourselves the Coo Ca Choo Girls, we did!'

I notice that the Coo Ca Choo Girls just
have peacock feathers covering themselves.

'Still got mine,' says Violet Rose, pointing to a straggly old feather stuck behind a painting of a castle. Her dressing table is scattered with make-up and perfume bottles. They all look used up. Everything looks used up ... old and dusty, including a photo of a young man in army uniform. I look back at Violet Rose before picking it up. The twinkle's gone out her eyes.

'Tell you wot, ducky,' she sighs. 'I'm not sure how long I'm going to be able to hold on to this lot if the rent goes up.'

'Can't you sell some of your diamonds?' I ask, without thinking. It's really none of my business, is it! But the idea of some old biddy – sitting on a fortune – getting kicked out of Lady Buxom because she doesn't have money to pay the rent seems crazy to me. But suddenly the twinkle's back.

'*Cor, ducky!* There's not a diamond amongst

this lot of old tat – all paste jewellery, it is! Just don't tell anyone around here,' she whispers. 'Think I'm *Lady Muck*, they do! But if the truth be told, I can't even afford to have me *mincers* done. Then, maybe that's a good thing – at least I won't be able to see what's going on around here when I've gone blind.'

'Mincers?' I ask.

'*Mince pies* – eyes!' she explains.

'What's wrong with your eyes?' I ask, going up to take a closer look at them. They look fine to me ... maybe a bit glassy.

Then she tells me she's got *'Whatchamacallit-Piggymantoes-Something-or-the-Other'* and that there's a clever doctor *'some place or the other'* who's the only one who can fix them with some *'radar type thingy or the other'*. It all sounds very confusing, but I think she means a *'laser'*. So I tell her about a friend of Gran's who had what I think are called *cataracts* removed by a quick laser treatment. Of course, I expect her to be excited by this good news. But she's not.

'Gran says her friend can now see craters on the moon with her new eyes,' I add, really wanting to cheer her up. But it doesn't.

'Wot I got,' she says, gloomily, 'is much more serious than that cattyrat thingy that a lot of old folk here have removed. My doc says I've got to get myself to *'God-knows-where'* and see this *'Radar-Doctor-Specialist-Chap'* . . . and that's going to cost a lot of money.'

'But Gran says you're very rich,' I let slip once more, and that makes Violet Rose's laughter lines wrinkle up.

'Cor, luvvy,' she chuckles, 'I've had a lot of boyfriends . . . a ton of laughs and a whole lot of life, but I've never had much money.' It sounds like a song the way she says it. And while I stand looking puzzled, she takes the photo from me, wipes the dust off it and tells me her story.

'That's my Freddy, poor love – never made it back from the war. Could have been a real lady myself and lived in that castle, over there.' She points to the painting on the wall.

'Instead, I'm in a hole with no room to swing a cat in and the only throne I'm ever going to sit on is that commode!' She points to a potty seat next to her bed. Her eyes fill with tears and I look away. Well, what else can I do!

'Just listen to me!' she sighs, dabbing her poor *'piggymantoes'* eyes. 'Keeping you here with my old stories! Off you go!'

As I make my way back to Gran, I start feeling really sad, and then start feeling *really* mad. Why should an old lady, who is going blind, have to worry about not having enough money to pay rent!

*It sucks!*

# Chapter Seven

Sophie's looking excited, waiting for me in the recreation room while some guy is talking to Gran.

'That's Blaire, he's great,' she whispers to me. 'And another thing, we've all been *compleeeeetely* wrong about Mrs Black. Blaire told me that she's an ex-nurse who's worked with refugee children in Africa. He says that she's an *incredibly* brave and caring person, but because she's lost so many people she's cared for, she copes with her sadness by pretending she doesn't care about anyone.'

'Well, she fooled me! I thought she was just plain psycho,' I say.

'*Noooo*, that's the way some people who've been exposed to war and horrid stuff are like,' says Sophie. 'Blaire says, it's like . . . shell-socked soldiers.'

She means *shell-shocked* soldiers.

'And the reason she uses all that make-up is to cover a face scar from a match settee.'

She means a machete – a long knife used in Africa.

'Blaire says, she's received bravery awards from Her Majesty. She's a *reeeal* hero!' Sophie's so psyched up! I give her a few seconds to catch her breath while I study Blaire. He looks a bit younger than my dad, and is trying far too hard to make himself look even younger by wearing clothes that look silly on him. A bit of his belly shows between his too-high T-shirt and too-low hipster pants. And for a hairdresser, his hair's a mess. OK, my hair has a mind of its own. But *his* hair just can't make up its mind *what* it wants to do. Some of it's blond, some of it's black, some of it's ginger, some of it's gelled . . . and some of it's spiked. To tell the truth, it looks as though a stressed-out cat has crash-landed on his head.

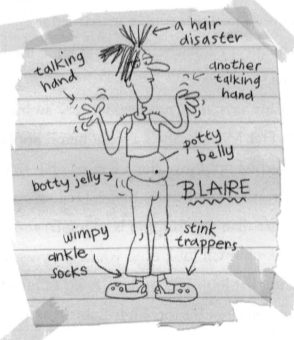

But Sophie doesn't agree.

'He's soooo cool and nice!' she whispers so he can't hear. 'He let me shampoo and dry. Mondays it's "Hair" and Thursdays it's "Pet Cures".'

She means pedicures – cutting toenails and yucky stuff.

My eyes drift back to Blaire, who seems as much of a talker as Mrs Black – only he uses his hands for much of it. 'No, she died last week . . . straight after her blow dry!' he tells Gran, and his hands go into a fanning action. 'Thought she looked a little peaky!' he whispers, and his hands press dents into his cheeks. Poor Gran looks quite squint trying to follow him.

'Are you listening or not!' scolds Sophie, and I jump to attention. 'He's soooo sweet with the old people – calls the old men "Gramps" and the old ladies "Gran" and comments on how nice they all look and what lovely hands and rings all the old grans have, and . . .'

I'm beginning to wonder if Sophie's picked up a talking bug the way she's jabbering on. So I say, 'Read my lips, Soph!' and go, 'T . . . M . . . I!'

For a second she's puzzled, then gets the message – *Too Much Information*!

She looks so funny when she gets cross . . . eyes flip upwards – mouth drops downwards. *What a Miss Sourpoops look!* But it never lasts with Sophie.

'Thanks, doll!' says Blaire, as he wafts by. 'See you tomorrow!'

'Byeeee!' says his biggest fan – all sweetness and smiles again.

I turn to Gran. 'Hungry?' she asks. I nod, and peer into her basket packed with our lunch. 'Julian should be with us soon,' she says as she unpacks some yummy-looking burgers, crisps and fruit juice. Just then we hear the heavy *thwack* of trainers coming down the corridor.

'Here's Julian now! And he's carrying a great big computer,' reports Sophie from the door.

'Hi!' gasps Julian, struggling in. 'I'm going to set up Mr Broomhall's computer so he can play some rad games.' I help him with the bulky tower. It has stickers all over it. One gives us the giggles:

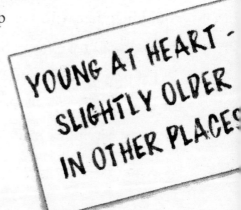

YOUNG AT HEART – SLIGHTLY OLDER IN OTHER PLACES

'I thought he wanted to send emails to his son in Australia,' says Sophie.

'No, he said his son's a *nincompoop* and he'd rather play computer games,' replies Julian. Gran bursts out laughing and spills some juice. 'These old folk are full of surprises!' she says.

*Just what I've been thinking!*

Over lunch, Sophie repeats *all* she's heard from Blaire about Mrs Black. Gran looks pretty unconvinced. I go, *'yeah, yeah, yeah!'* But Julian says, 'What did I say! I *told* you she was mysterious, didn't I? Gosh, I'd like to see her scar!' I wait for him to get over himself and then tell them about Violet Rose, and how I wish we could help her with her money problems.

'Well, can't we?' asks Sophie.

'I suppose so, but *how*?' I ask, looking to Gran for inspiration ... *and get it*! She's wearing the artyfarty earrings I made out of bottle tops for her birthday – an idea I got from a book I have on recycling.

'I KNOW!' I yell – cos that's what I do when I'm excited – I yell, I don't talk:

'WE CAN MAKE ÜBER COOL STUFF OUT OF RECYCLED JUNK AND SELL IT AT A MARKET OR SET UP STALL IN THE MALL!'

'You're shouting,' says Sophie, 'but it's a super idea.'

'I've got loads of computer bits we can use,' says Julian.

'And I can make beanie hats and leg blankies out of old pullovers,' adds Sophie.

'I'm sure there are enough baldies here who will buy your beanies,' jokes Gran.

While we're chuckling over *'Beanies for Baldies'*, I imagine all the money we're going to raise for Violet Rose. I can see it piling up!

'We can call it the HELP VIOLET ROSE FUND!' I suggest.

Gran raises her juice. 'Here's to the Help Violet Rose Fund!' she says.

*'To the Help Violet Rose Fund!'* we all toast together.

# Chapter Eight

For the next couple of days we're kept busy making really cool things for our sale. Sometimes, we're at Sophie's house, which actually *rocks* from the pounding of electric guitars coming from her brothers' room.

Tom-Tom's made it impossible for us to work at home because he grabs everything he can reach. But Julian's place is great because both his parents work and we have the place to ourselves. *Plus* Julian makes *really* chunky energy drinks, using bananas, fruit yogurt and cereal.

And we need it for all the work we're doing. Honestly, there's just *noooo* limit to what we can make from the junk we've collected –

Bottle top and can tab jewellery

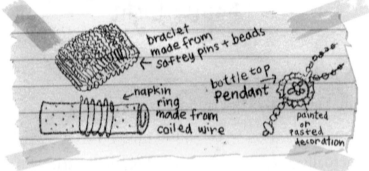

bracelet made from ← saftey pins + beads

←napkin ring made from coiled wire

bottle top pendant

painted or pasted decoration

Beanies and leg blankies made out of the charity shop jerseys

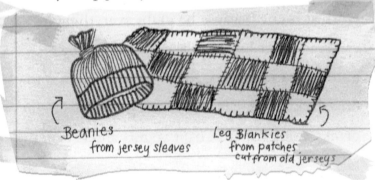

Beanies from jersey sleaves

Leg Blankies from patches cut from old jerseys

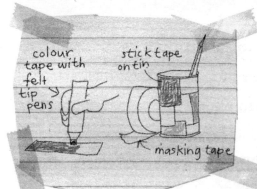

colour tape with felt tip pens

stick tape on tin

masking tape

Tin can and masking tape containers for pencils

Secret safes made by hollowing out the pages of old books

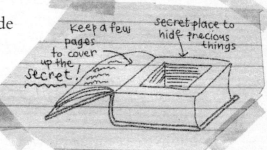

Keep a few pages to cover up the secret!

secret place to hide precious things

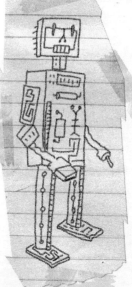

Julian's truly awesome sculptures built from computer scraps

And the good news is that Julian's dad, who owns a computer shop in the local mall, has arranged for us to put up our stall outside his shop. It's a massively busy shopping centre so we really ought to make stacks of money. Especially on a Saturday morning *and* when people see that it's for a good cause.

The bad news comes later when Gran says, 'I heard today that Mrs Black has put up the rent. I reckon most of the old folk will be helped out by their families. But I don't think Vi has any family – poor thing. How are you guys doing with your sale?'

I tell her that we're all set for Saturday, and describe our goods. 'Great! I'll support you. I want one of your bottle-top pendants to go with my super earrings,' says Gran.

Saturday morning comes and Julian's mum helps get our stuff to the mall in her huge 4x4. By the time it's all displayed, I'm sweaty. But it looks great. We've even made a banner out of recycled plastic bags – 'In aid of the HELP VIOLET ROSE FUND' it says.

But no sooner is it put up when Sophie comes running from the loo, all flushed and panting. *'Take it down! Take it down!'* she yells, and starts pulling at the banner. 'I've just seen the old folk climbing out of the Lady Buxom bus . . . *and Violet Rose is with them!'*

She's right, we don't want Violet Rose to see that we are raising funds for her. It's meant to be a surprise, and the last thing we want to do is to make her feel like a charity case in front of her better-off friends. So we stuff the banner in a box and hope our winning smiles will attract customers. But after a while, we can't even keep that up – *everyone's walking by without even glancing at our table!*

'Maybe I should stand on the table and dance,' suggests Sophie, looking as though she's about to cry. Then, without any warning, Julian starts advertising *by mouth* . . . very loudly:

OK, now let me explain Julian's voice – it's starting to break, you see? So it's all over the place – deep like his dad's one minute, then, suddenly without any warning, it goes *waaay* high and squeaky like his mum's. And right now, it's not doing our sales much good. In fact, people are actually starting to *avoid* us – as though we're a group of crazy Bible-bashing freaks trying to convert them to our Church of Loonies.

Only one person comes to the table – pushed there in her wheelchair by an old geezer. It's Violet Rose and the Major!

'Hrgrumph!' grunts the Major. 'If it isn't our young friends!'

'Hello, duckies! What's all this, then?' says Violet Rose, opening up one of our book safes. 'Cor, ain't this a good idea, Archie,' she says to the Major, who passes me one of Sophie's beanies and says, 'I'll take this!' Then adds,

'And the *bookwhatsit* for Miss Rose.'

He explains to Violet Rose that it's a gift and she holds it tightly, giving me one of her antique smiles. Just then, Blaire appears, pushing an old man in a wheelchair. Sophie's very pleased to see Blaire. He's wearing another of his winning outfits!

'Don't you think these are cool, Blaire?' she coos, showing him her beanies. But he's more interested in the book that Violet Rose is clutching. I see him pick up one from the table and study it. '*Mmmm* . . . foxy!' he says, then chucks it down.

*Creep!*

Soon, a few more old folk from the home join in. We make a few sales but most pick up and put down again. And that's the way it goes. By lunch time, we're ready to give up and spend what little money we've made to buy a burger, chips and Coke each. Instead, Julian's mum brings us vegetarian wraps from the health food shop and tries to cheer us up.

'That's business for you,' she says. 'Some days . . . profit, some days . . . loss.'

We look miserably at all the stuff left unsold.

'And some days,' groans Sophie, 'just plain suck!'

# Chapter Nine

Bingo Night at the old folks' home is Gran's idea. Having *The Test Icicles* to provide entertainment is mine. And it's not a good one.

We spend the money made from our sales on tea, crisps and biscuits, and give away the rest of our stuff as prizes. At teatime we count the money made from ticket sales, and we're only a tiny bit better off than we were from our miserable mall sale.

'I have an idea,' chirps Sophie. But I can't hear what it is, because right then *The Test Icicles* blast off with one of their brain-bashing numbers.

'*Kill the Sucker! Kill him! Kill him!*' they scream.

Some old folk tap happily on tables – their hearing aids turned off. Some look as though they've been plugged into a million volts! Gran tries to get the band's attention by miming a

*'turn it down'* action. But it's no use.

Suddenly, Mrs Black storms in and marches over to the band. Her tries to get them to drop the volume are misunderstood and they turn it up instead. Mrs Black attempts to cut off their power supply by pulling fiercely at an electric cable. Ethan stops singing and starts a frenzied tug of war with her. It's a no-brainer! Like a

battle of strength between a praying mantis and a banshee on steroids! Mrs Black gives the winning tug that lifts Ethan off his bare feet and into the air. When he lands, he's on top of her. Dopily, he lifts his head, yawns and throws up. It looks as though he's had lunch at Raymoondo Banergees's Curry Cafe . . . and washed it down with far too much beer. If Mrs Black doesn't murder him, I bet his dad'll do the job for her.

'*Kill the Sucker! Kill him! Kill him!*' *The Test Icicles* carry on shouting . . .

. . . unplugged.

# Chapter Ten

'Mrs Black is dead against having a visiting author at the Lady Buxom home,' says Gran. 'Not after that poor boy got sick all over her.'

An *Author's Talk* is Sophie's idea, and she suggests Polly Hamsbottom, a local children's author and illustrator of the *Puffin Muffin* series.

'Lots of grandparents, parents and children will pay to hear Polly Hamsbottom talk,' she tells us. 'She can sign her books and we'll make tons of money on sales. Our school's done author's visits and bought a computer for the library from the sales.'

'That's true, Gran,' I add. The fact is – we're desperate. The Help Violet Rose Fund has become much more than a school project to us. It's become our *dream*.

'OK,' says Gran, 'I'll see if I can talk Walkie-Talkie into it.'

When Gran comes back with the good news that it's on, Sophie finds out how to contact Polly Hamsbottom through our local library. And as it turns out, Nadia, the children's librarian knows her personally, and gives us her email address.

Together, we write:

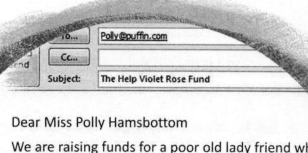

To... Polly@puffin.com

Cc...

Subject: The Help Violet Rose Fund

Dear Miss Polly Hamsbottom

We are raising funds for a poor old lady friend who
needs to get her eyes fixed and we wonder if you
would like to help us by doing an Author's Talk and
read your <u>brilliant</u> Puffin Muffin stories to a group
of all ages. We plan to sell signed copies of your books
(if you will bring some) and share the money with you.

Your Fans

Alistair D'arcy McDermott

Sophie Ross

Julian Pettifer

A few days later we receive a handwritten letter
AND a drawing of Puffin Muffin.

Dear Alistair, Sophie and Julian

I *LOVE* making public appearances
so I'd be thrilled to help you out.
Send me all the details and how many
books you'd like me to bring for signing.
yours cuddlingly

Puffin Muffin

We think it's a bit weird to get a letter from Puffin Muffin and not Polly Hamsbottom. But Sophie says it's because, over time, some authors and their characters get all mixed up.

And she couldn't be more right!

On the evening of the *Author's Talk*, we are waiting at the entrance of the Lady Buxom Home for our famous local children's author and illustrator to arrive. But instead of a lady, out steps a large fluffy creature from an ancient car that looks like a Tudor house on wheels.

*Crikey!* It's Puffin Muffin!

*'Hell-oooooo, little one-ees!'* comes a booming voice through a big plastic yellow beak.

'Hello . . . welcome!' we reply, half gagged by surprise.

'See . . . *boooooks!'* cries Puffin Muffin, opening the back of her car.

We jump into action and each grab a pile. I avoid looking at the other two because, *if* I do, I know I will crack up and drop the books – *not a good idea!* I hear a stifled giggle in Sophie's voice as she leads the way saying, 'This way . . . Miss Hams . . . bottom!'

*'Me, Puffin Muffin!'* says Puffin Muffin, sounding all hurt.

'Alistair D'arcy McDermott,' I say to myself, while steering clear of the enormous fluffy bottom bouncing in front of me, *'what have we done!'*

Exactly!

Puffin Muffin, who really looks more like a yeti, scares the little children silly so that some parents are forced to leave with them. Those who stay look embarrassed out of their minds when Puffin Muffin tells us all to jump up and dance to the Puffin Muffin Song –

'Flip flop – let's all go Shufflin!
Wiggle waggle – our fluffy Muffin!
Hip hop – till we start Puffin!
Let's all do – the Puffin Muffin!'

Even the old folk think it's too silly for words and start digging into the refreshments before it's time. Then one little boy gives Puffin Muffin a shove on her fat bottom so that Puffin Muffin's head falls off. And there stands Polly Hamsbottom – sweaty and furious. In fact, she plain loses it and gives the little boy a kick in the pants. It's not a serious kick, but the little kid howls like he's been crippled for life. Suddenly, it's like a daytime TV show with everyone shouting at each other. The little kid's parents snatch him up and call Polly Hamsbottom *'A vicious child abuser'*. Then Polly Hamsbottom calls them a name that I'm sure Puffin Muffin would *never* use!

It's more than a disaster! It's a total *meltdown!*

The remaining parents collect their crying
children and leave while the old folk start
stuffing their pockets with biscuits and crisps
and toddle off to their rooms.

We've manage to sell *one* book . . . to Sailor
Flynn.

'That's only because he fancies Polly
Hamsbottom,' says Sophie.

'Or, Puffin Muffin,' says Julian.

At least we have *something* to laugh about.

# Chapter Eleven

The next day is Friday and we're at Raymoondo's Curry Cafe.

'I give up!' sighs Sophie. 'We're *never* going to make enough money to help poor Violet Rose.'

'She'll be booted out of Lady Buxom and have to live under a bridge with winos,' says Julian. The thought's too awful!

'*We can't give up!*' I say, firmly. I'm really disappointed with them for being so negative. But I suppose this *has* all been my idea so I can't really blame them.

Still . . .

*'I won't give up!'* I yell. I'm being a bit overdramatic and manage to drop my date ball in my Coke.

'Give up what?' asks Raymoondo, coming over to our table with a cloth. 'I hope not my delicious date balls!' I start telling him about the difficult time we're having trying to raise funds for Violet Rose.

'Violet Rose, you say?' He repeats her name as though he might know her. *And he does!*

'Many years ago, when I was in show business,' he tells us, 'I was a supporting act for the *Coo Ca Choo Girls*.' I try to imagine him with naked ladies waving their peacock feathers about and smile. 'No, as true as Bob!' he says, taking down a photo from the wall, 'See, that's me – the Great Raymoondo Banergee – Reader of Minds and Teller of Fortunes.' He taps the framed photo of a dark, handsome man with hypnotic eyes, dressed in Indian clothes.

'Now, I want you to tell me what's on your minds!' he says, sitting down with us.

'I thought you said you can read minds,' jokes Sophie.

'*So I can! So I can!*' he replies. 'And what I see is that something *verrry* serious is troubling you all.'

So I tell him, and when he's heard the full story, he says, 'What you guys need is a little show biz – there's *nothing* like it to pull in the crowds and make big bucks.' The three of us exchange looks – and you *don't* have to be a mind reader to know that we haven't a clue about *show biz*. But, as it turns out, we don't have to, because Raymoondo sits back and gives us a broad, dashing, show biz smile and says, 'Ah, my young friends, there's nothing, absolutely *nothing* I would not do for a *Coo Ca Choo Girl*!'

# Chapter Twelve

Here's the plan!

*We advertise in our local newspaper – 'An Evening with The Great Raymoondo Banergee – Reader of Minds and Teller of Fortunes.'* There'll be a curry dinner and then entertainment. Sophie, Julian and I will dress up as Indian waiters, and serve the guests. Gran will take care of the money at the door.

Also, I'll design a leaflet that can work as an ad as well. Julian will scan and print it out – I suggest that it includes the words *'A Fund*

*Raising Event'*. Sophie will make photocopies, and we'll hand them out on the street outside the Curry Cafe a few days before the big event.

*Billowing Bloomers!* I'm so hyped that I can hardly sleep. And everyone from our families wants to come when they see our ad in the *Village News*.

'I rather like show biz,' says Julian, admiring his reflection in the Curry Cafe window. Sophie and I smile as he skips off after people, thrusting leaflets into their hands. This community project thingy has really shown us what we can do together. I mean, we may have started as a group, but now we're a tight, butt-kicking team.

It takes us just over an hour to hand out all the leaflets.

'*Refreshments!*' announces Raymoondo, serving us drinks on a tray. '*Bombay Crush!*' he tells us – a coconut milk smoothie with a sprinkle of nutmeg. They're strange but delicious, leaving white moustaches clinging to the top of our lips.

I hurry Julian, who takes ages with everything he drinks or eats. 'We've got to get to Gran's for a costume fitting,' I remind them.

We say '*Al Vida!*' – which is 'goodbye' in Hindi – to Raymoondo as we leave.

Gran has made us red cummerbunds that we'll wear with our dark school trousers and white shirts. But when we try on our outfits, she decides that we need black bow ties and red turbans to really nail the Eastern look.

While she's sewing, we watch a bit of telly. It seems like ages since we've been able to relax. But no sooner are we into a movie when Gran calls, 'Let's see how you look in these!'

We don't look half daft. But so what . . . it's fun.

*Bollywood, here we come!*

# Chapter Thirteen

The Curry Cafe is booked out. 'Standing room only!' laughs Gran. It makes me so happy to hear her say that old Vi's *'going to be sailing'* after tonight. But when I think of tonight, I get butterflies.

*Nothing must go wrong!*

Mum suggests I have a rest then take a bath before we set off. Later, when Susan from next door arrives to babysit Tom-Tom, I'm clean all over and look like a Bollywood lover boy in my outfit.

'Aren't you just the handsome Maharajah!' chaffs Sue when I open the door.

I turn as red as my cummerbund. She's a babe – Sue – but too old for me. Sophie's the right age, but then we're more like brother and sister, and you don't think about your sister in *that* way, do you?

I give Tom-Tom a goodbye kiss, but then have to run to the bathroom to wash my face again after he leaves a gooey streak on my chin. Mum and Dad wait at the gate for me.

We can really walk down to the Curry Cafe, but there's *no way* that I'm going to be seen in public in this gear. So Dad agrees to go by car.

*'You're the jewel in my lotus!'* he sings to Mum as we climb in the car. I give him the thumbs down.

*There's going to be no singing and hip shaking from him tonight!*

When we arrive, Gran's already there collecting cash from people who have to queue outside to get in. The butterflies in my tummy have turned into bats and it's only when I see Sophie that I feel a little less nervous.

'Where's Julian?' I ask, looking around the cafe, which is starting to fill up.

'He's in the loo. I think he's been five times already!' she tells me.

'Are you nervous?' I ask.

'Yes, but in a nice way. Not like "exam" nervous,' she replies, tightening her cummerbund. So we're standing there chatting when Julian walks up.

'Your fly's undone,' I tell him.

'*Oh, nooo!*' and he buckles over – hopping and bopping, trying to find his zipper.

'Now that's show biz!' laughs Sophie.

The place is almost packed when Mrs Banergee calls us into the kitchen, where she shows us how to carry a plate of curry without spilling it or burning our hands.

Raymoondo's wearing Mrs Banergee's frilly apron over his stage clothes. He is made up around the eyes and looks quite scary, although he's in a jolly mood.

'*There's no business like show business,*' he warbles as he dishes up from of a big pot of delicious-smelling curry. Mrs B puts plates on to the napkins folded in our hands and opens the door for us. We stroll out, looking like three extras in a Bollywood movie. I'm so nervous about not spilling that I almost trip over my own feet, but manage not to screw up. Sophie looks like she's been waitressing all her life. And Julian looks as though he might need to go again!

With every new serving we get better, and soon we're dashing about until everyone has been served. While the eating's going on, Mrs B gives us our dinner in the kitchen. It's a special dish she's made just for us – *Sooji* with sweet cooked semolina. *Really yummy!*

We eat carefully so that nothing spills on our costumes and listen to the happy sound of people in the cafe. Then the moment arrives and Raymoondo takes off his apron and turns before our very eyes into – *The Great Raymoondo Banergee, Reader of Minds and Teller of Fortunes.*

We follow him into the cafe and stand to the side. The lights dim, the music is turned down and the show starts.

'Someone is thinking about changing jobs,' he tells the audience, in a deep mysterious voice.

'He's right! I am!' shouts a young man from the back.

'You will be a great success in your new job!' he assures the astounded young man.

'And you, dear lady, must stop worrying about your health,' he says to a rather large lady sitting in the front. 'You eat much too quickly, and that's what causes your terrible botty-burps,' he tells her. The lady looks relieved and everyone has a good laugh.

The mind reading goes on for a while and is very entertaining. Then Raymoondo suddenly stops and seems to go into a deep trance.

'Aaaaaaaaah!' his voice quavers. 'There has been much trouble. I see it! It comes from . . . where?' Slowly, he turns around and approaches me.

*Freaky!* Sophie takes hold of my hand.

'Ah, yes, indeed,' he mumbles, 'I see much trouble and strife . . . but also plenty bucks!'

I feel Sophie's hand relax in mine.

'*Aaaaaaaaah!*' he continues. '*Daaarknesss!* Beware of the treacherous Horned Heart!'

I grip Sophie's hand and out of the corner of my eye I see Julian disappear into the loo.

'*Aaaaaaaaaaaaaah!*' moans Raymoondo. '*Dangerrrrrr . . . a fierce battle of good against evil . . . light against the dark! But the powerful Pink Tiger will defeat the evil Horned Heart.*'

My hand feels squidgy in Sophie's. Suddenly, Raymoondo's eyes flare open and bore into mine. I feel as though I'm falling into a cavern of darkness as he holds me in his power. I grip Sophie's hand so tightly that it squooshes right out of mine.

You can hear a pin drop . . .

'*Aaaaaaaah!*' But this time it's a relaxed sigh and I feel my fear lift as he calmly continues, 'Peace will return to the Land of the Old. Indeed, furthermore *and* henceforth there will be light where there was darkness, happiness where there was despair – and you, my dear Prince (he means me!), shall inherit a castle.'

For a few seconds there's silence, and then applause as Raymoondo bows and shuffles backwards into the kitchen. A minute later he returns, fully recovered from his strange trance, and with a clap of the hands announces:

'Now, ladies and gentleman –

*Currrrrrrryoooooake!*'

*Oh no!* I see my father getting up from the table.

# Chapter Fourteen

I can't believe it!

We've made an amazing £1200 – but we're going to be very private about it. We'll slip the cash into an envelope and hand it to Violet Rose without anyone knowing. Gran suggests we say it comes from a secret admirer, and that ought to make it easier for Violet Rose to accept. And in a way it has – coming from Raymoondo and all. He's obviously gaga over the *Coo Ca Choo Girls* – couldn't stop talking about them while we were helping him clear up after the show. Mrs B looked as though she wanted to hit him over the head with her chapatti pan!

'So what do you think Raymoondo meant with all his *Aaaaaaahing* and *Dangerrrrr* and *Daaaarknesss*?' Sophie wants to know, when we see each other the next day.

'He *did* say where there was darkness there will be light,' adds Julian.

'How do you know?' I ask him. 'You were in the loo most of the time.'

'Well, it was *frrrrightfully spoooooky*!' says Julian, doing an Indian accent that sounds more Scottish.

We're with Gran in the recreation room, waiting for the art class to end so that we can see Violet Rose on her own.

'Why don't you help Julian get Mr

Broomhall's computer back to him,' Gran suggests, 'and be careful! Mr Wimpole, the janitor, is touching up some paintwork along the corridors.'

'Eeeek! It's "Nails" today!' Sophie cries, and darts off to the hair salon.

Julian and I stumble to Mr Broomhall's room to deliver his computer. It feels heavier with all the games Julian's loaded for him. Mr Broomhall's thrilled. He especially digs *Roadkill* – which is strange, because he's the most gentle old man you could ever meet. But once he gets going with *Roadkill*, you should see him. He becomes *demon* possessed!

Got you, you rotter!
Take THAT, you swine!

Julian and I leave him, happily killing victims on his screen. Then as we're heading back to the recreation room we stumble into Mrs Black, who comes clomping down the corridor – a phone pressed to her ear. She doesn't even realize that she's almost flattened us with her big boots.

'Listen, wimp!' we hear her hiss into her phone. 'I want a proper job done this time! And if there's a mess, you clean it up. *Get it?*'

When she's out of hearing distance, I say to Julian, '*That* sounded suspicious!'

'Oh, I'm sure she was talking to that Wimpole guy your gran was telling us about – the one that's doing the painting.'

Well . . . umm . . . maybe.

Back in the recreation room the old folk are finishing up. Violet Rose has painted some sad, droopy blue flowers in a bowl.

'Have you ever seen such a sorry bowl of flowers, ducky?' she asks me.

'Arf, arf!' coughs the Major, getting ready for a joke. 'It's your blue period, Violet . . . you and Picasso!'

'You can say that again,' replies Violet Rose, gloomily. 'I'm *feeling* blue, all right.'

Gran drops a hint. 'Not for long, Vi . . . not for long!' Then when Violet Rose is not looking, she slips me the envelope, which I tuck safely into my jacket pocket.

Julian wants to wheel Violet Rose to her room, so I let him. We find Sophie at the hairdresser's painting stars on some very wrinkly old toes.

'Coming then, Soph?' I ask. She looks to see what Blaire has to say.

'Go on then, luv,' he says, 'Monday's *"Hair"*, remember.'

Sophie jumps up and joins us, leaving the old lady with veined feet and flowery toenails snoring in her chair. *Phwaor!* I'm glad I didn't get the job in the salon. It's been great helping Gran, and our last fundraiser was a blast. Now I can't wait to put a smile on Violet Rose's sad face.

*'Blow me down!'* is all she can say when she sees what's in the envelope.

'Now you don't have to worry about your rent,' I tell her. With trembling hands, she takes my hand, letting the money fall on the floor. 'Hey, you've got to look after this!' I say, picking it up. I look around for a safe place and see the book safe that the Major bought her, lying on her potty-chair.

'Here!' I say, slipping the bundle of notes into the secret hollow of the book and closing it. 'No one will find it now,' I tell her and hand it over.

It's such a precious gift that she holds it tightly against her heart, and her eyes sparkle like real diamonds.

'So, Miss Rose, who's the secret admirer, then?' asks Sophie, swishing the peacock feather around the room.

'Lord knows!' giggles Violet Rose, but glancing at the photo of her wartime boyfriend.

'Well, someone must think that you're very special,' I tease.

'You'd better believe it, ducky,' says Violet Rose.

And the Coo Ca Choo Girls smile naughtily down from the wall at her.

# Chapter Fifteen

I love blowing farty sounds on Tom-Tom's
tummy. It makes him clutch my hair and shake
like a jelly with the giggles. We've got just over
a week and then it's back to school. So, I'm
chilling out with him. Each day Gran pops in
and tells me, *'Vi sends her love.'* So, I guess
everything is fine at the Lady Buxom Home
for Seniors.

## AND THEN IT HAPPENS!

'You won't believe it! They cleaned out the whole place last night! Every bit of gold they could lay their hands on,' Gran runs in, telling us. 'Television sets, hairdryers . . . even those machines for measuring blood pressure! *Gone!*'

'Oh, no!' gasps Mum, 'I hope no one was hurt.'

'There was no need for that. They were all asleep – well, *drugged* when it happened,' says Gran. 'A really professional job – someone must have got into the kitchen and slipped some medication into the soup, or maybe the pudding – you know how the old folk like their pudding, spiked or not. The night staff wondered why everything was so quiet. I can just imagine the lot of them watching telly while the place was being ransacked.'

*My first thought is Violet Rose's money!*

I call Sophie and then Julian. At first they

think I'm joking, but when I tell them I'm
going to see for myself if Violet Rose is OK,
they agree to meet me at the home. I leave
immediately with Gran, and wait for Sophie
and Julian at the entrance. When they arrive, we
dash off to Violet Rose's room. On the way,
Sophie tries the door to the hair salon to see
what's missing. The door's locked. When we
reach Violet Rose, she's sitting with the book
safe on her lap. It's open and emptied.

Violet Rose is devastated.

'Took the whole bundle! Knew what they
were doing too! Didn't touch a single piece of
my old junk,' she tells us, stroking her old
brooch and necklace with a trembling hand.
Then she looks at me through watery eyes, and
says, 'Had a damn good sleep, though.'

She's lost everything . . . but not her humour.
*Blast!* If the low-life scum who stole from her

was here, all three of us would stomp on his nasty head!

'But how did anyone know where to look?' asks Sophie. 'That's supposed to be a secret place.'

Blaire crosses my mind. *'Mmmm . . . foxy!'* Hah! I thought his interest in the book safe at our sale was a bit suspect. We leave Violet Rose and find Gran in the reception area surrounded by a group of worried residents.

'Has Mrs Black reported this to the police?' asks one in a shaken voice.

'Haven't seen her this morning,' says another.

'The hairdresser chap hasn't turned up either and I look a mess,' says an old lady with sticky-out hair.

'Gruwmf! And the damn office is locked!' snorts the Major.

'Let's go!' I whisper to Julian, and we head off to look around.

'Hey! Wait for me!' calls Sophie, doing up her laces.

Gran calls after us, 'Don't wander about. The police will be here soon and I don't want you to get in their way!'

'We won't, Gran,' I call back. *We'll be one step ahead!*

Sophie, being the smallest, agrees to climb through the office window that's been left a bit open. But before we can lift her up, I spot Mr Wimpole, the janitor, in the parking lot.

'What you want from the office?' he asks grumpily when we ask if he can open up for us.

Quickly, Julian starts to improvise. 'I promised Mrs Black I'd defrag her computer,' he says.

'What's wrong with her fragging computer?' asks Wimpole. I've never seen such a tangle of eyebrows, sideburns and nose hairs in my life!

He looks like a hairy turnip.

'It may have a bug,' says Julian.

'Bugs, hey? Well I don't want any bugs around this place. It's already full of damp and woodworm.' Then without a word he heads off, and we follow him to the office.

'Something fishy going on here, if you ask me,' he says, when finds the right key and opens up. The office looks a mess – paper everywhere . . . and the safe's open. Sophie and I start looking for clues. Automatically, Julian switches on the desktop. It takes ages to boot up. Meanwhile, I look through a magazine I find lying in the wastepaper basket – *Golden Years*. It's full of ads for old people's homes. I flip through it and my eyes go straight to a small black and white ad.

*'Trained Nurse with Nursing Home Management Skills Seeks Employment.'*

Underneath is a photo . . . of Mrs Black. But there's no contact number, only a P.O. Box address.

'That's odd,' I hear Julian say. He's going through Mrs Black's emails. Only, there are no emails – not in the 'inbox' nor in the 'sent'.

'Try deleted files,' suggests Sophie. And I'm impressed.

It doesn't take him long to sift through the latest deleted emails. *Bingo!* He finds one that will send me on my greatest mission yet. Julian reads it.

catstreaks@yaya.com

Cc...

Subject: rendezvous at noon

Will meet you tomorrow on platform 6
Paddington, 12.00 noon sharp.
DON'T SCREW UP!
Mum

We can see when it was sent – Thurs, 5.30 p.m. – yesterday.

And who it was sent to – catstreaks@yaya.com. I can guess who that is!

'Blaire!' I say.

'Oh no!' Sophie whimpers. 'He's soooo nice!'

'We'll have to see about that!' I say, and quickly jot down the details. 'Come on!'

Gran's still at reception trying to calm down upset old folk.

'The police are taking ages,' she sighs when she sees us. 'I think you children had better go home.'

'No, Gran!' I say, explaining what we discovered on Mrs Black's computer. Gran's sharp – she can put two and two together, so I don't have to go into much detail. 'If we hurry we can catch them!' I plead.

'I'll handle this,' Gran says. 'Now, I want you to go home and let your mum know that I'm heading for Paddington. I'll have my phone on.'

'But Gran,' I warn her, 'they could be dangerous!'

'That's why I want you at home,' she replies. 'Off you go now, and take Sophie and Julian with you.' She looks at her watch and says, 'I've got just under an hour!' Then she slings her bag over her shoulder and heads for her car.

'Cripes, your gran is so cool!' says Julian as we watch her jog towards the car park.

'Yeah, how she can run on those shoes is just amazing,' says Sophie, 'I hope she's going to be all right.'

Well, that does it!

# Chapter Sixteen

From the back seat, I hear Gran talking to Mum on her mobile –

'Don't worry, darling, I can handle them,' she says. I stick an ear out and listen. 'I told Al to go home, he should be with you any minute now. Right, I'll call when I've dealt with them.'

It's a good thing that Gran's so untidy. She's left me a picnic blanket to hide under. Sneaking into the back of the car while she was busy getting out her car keys was another matter. And if she had not left the boot

unlocked, I wouldn't be here at all.

Now, all I've got to do is shadow her . . . all the way to platform six.

Suddenly, the car jolts to a stop and I wait until Gran climbs out. Then, quietly, I lift up the unlocked boot door and sneak out. I stay low, breaking into a funny, chimpanzee shuffle with my back all bent and my hands almost scraping the ground. Some people clear out of the way. I guess they think I'm a junkie-kid, drugged out of his mind. But as long as it keeps Gran from

seeing me, I don't care if I've got to walk on
my hands.

It's only when I enter the station that I can
straighten up. So far, so good! It helps that
Gran's moving like a guided missile towards her
target. There's no looking back or anything that
will distract her when she's in her Yubiwaza
mode. The mass of people criss-crossing the
main hall makes it hard for me to keep up with
her. But I make sure I can see the platform
numbers and head for six.

The large station clock above says it's 11.45 p.m. There's fifteen minutes to find Mrs Black and her accomplice! I can't get over Blaire being her son, though. He's certainly weird. But nasty . . . violent . . . huh, *that* I'm about to find out!

As I approach the entrance to platform six, I spot Gran. She's scanning the crowd like Robocop. Suddenly, she pushes through a group of tourists blocking her way. She's seen something!

I see her too!

'Mrs Black, I arrest you!' I hear Gran shout. I rush forward, fighting my way through people pouring out from the train that's just arrived. I feel myself being carried in the current of bodies – caught between a lady in a thick woolly coat and a fat man in a striped suit.

By the time I break free and reach the action, Gran is rolling on the ground with Mrs Black. The crowd give way to form a ring around them. Mrs Black manages to get on to her high-heel ankle boots and starts circling around Gran. She reminds me of a crazed rooster in a cock fight – terrifying in her silky red bomber jacket and black tights. Gran looks magnificent as she gets up – like a great big tiger in her fleecy pink tracksuit.

*Of course, Raymoondo's prediction – The Pink Tiger!*

Well, it's going to take more than a bad strip cartoon character like Mrs Black to beat a Yubiwaza champ! With her strong legs slightly bent, and her arms bowed in a crescent moon position, Gran takes up the deadly stance of *The Black Dragon* – poised to strike and deliver *The Death Touch*. I hold my breath, as she sways like a cobra on her platforms. The suspense is killing.

'You have two choices, Mrs Black!' says Gran in a calm, steady voice. 'Either you come easily with me, or you go down hard!'

Sneering, Mrs Black spits out the side of her mouth, and that's when Blaire pushes his way forward. 'Oh, Mum!' he cries. 'Don't spit! It's so yucky!'

Well, if I had a mother like that I'd be, like, *sooooooo* embarrassed!

'Shut your mealy mouth and hand me my bag!' she yells at him. He obeys her like a wimpy little dog and out of her bag, she pulls her lipstick – only it's not lipstick! It's one of those deadly disguised weapons advertised on Tellymart shows:

**'The 350,000 volt Lipstick Stun Gun plus LED Flashlights to temporarily blind your victim!'**

*'Watch out, Gran!'* I shout.
*Mistake!*

Gran turns around, giving Mrs Black the advantage. With lipstick in hand, she charges Gran – making for her neck.

'*Look out!*' cries the crowd. And with lightning speed, Gran spins on the heel of her right shoe and with an outstretched fist she knocks the silly weapon clean out of Mrs Black's hand. The crowd cheer like football fans seeing their team scoring a goal.

But it's not over yet!

Mrs Black lets out a blood-curdling shriek, and goes in for the kill – her long talons recklessly cutting the air as she goes for Gran. Immediately, Gran does a zero-gravity-backwards-tilt, giving Mrs Black a clear path to follow through on a badly judged move. She tries to brake. Instead, Gran trips her up and Mrs Black comes skidding towards me.

*Good! Gran wins . . .*

*NOT!*

Slowly, Mrs Black raises her sweaty face from the ground . . . and recognizes me.

*Eeek!*

Before I can get away she leaps up and grabs hold of my collar. I struggle to free myself, and yank the sleeve off her jacket – exposing a muscular arm that's just twitching for action. And that's when I see it – a tattooed heart with horns. In the centre are the words: 'SOD OFF!'

*Rocky Horrors! She's the Horned Heart!*

'Let go of that child!' I hear a soft but firm voice say from behind. And when Mrs Black doesn't, I see a collection box come crashing down on her head. I know it's a collection box because of the *'Women Pacifists Against Child Abuse'* message on it. For a moment I want to burst out laughing, but the Horned Heart is scrambling to her feet again.

*The monster's indestructible!*

She stands sneering and snorting, snarling and spitting like a mad bull, gathering its strength before one last, final attempt to obliterate Gran. But before she moves a muscle, Gran walks casually over . . . and with a quick, finger-flicking action under Mrs Black's nose, she brings down the Horned Heart . . . like a felled tree.

*Thwump!*

Seeing his mum defeated, Blaire tries to give us the slip, but is slowed down by his ridiculously large bag that bangs against his legs as he runs. I go after him, not knowing what I'll do when I catch up.

Now, you've got to see this in slow motion –

Blaire's making the progress of an overloaded, knock-kneed camel – so I come from behind –

make a low dive – and grab him around the legs. He manages one step forwards – but I hold on – then collapses in a great big muddle of legs, arms and bag handles. I don't know what is what until I hear his sobs.

'Boo-hoo! Mum made me do it! I didn't want to rob any of those old people! I can't take any more of her abuse!'

He looks so pathetic that I actually feel sorry for him, especially when the police take him away. Mrs Black needs an ambulance with armed guards to get her to hospital. Gran says she'll recover. 'But you, young man . . .' she scolds. Then, when she sees I'm fine she opens her arms and yells, *'Oh come here!'* and lifts me clean off my feet.

As we pass under the clock, it turns: 12:05.

'Well, that didn't take too long, did it!' says Gran, pulling her tracksuit straight. 'Now let's grab some lunch!'

We pass the sweet lady with her collection box and I take a coin from my wallet and pop it in. She offers me a sticker and I stick it on Gran's pink top.

'Gee, thanks!' says Gran, patting it. 'This means so much more to me than my Yubiwaza Gold Medal!'

I look up to see if she's kidding.

She isn't!

# Chapter Seventeen

Some of the headlines are sensational.

There are stories about Mrs Black and her son, Blaire. How they've been ripping off pensioners while employed at all these old folks' homes. The police say that the *Horned Heart*, as Mrs Black is known in the gang world, has been giving them the slip for the past year. Some of the things they've done are quite diabolical!

*No! I'm not going to describe them to you!* Well, OK, then . . . just one:

Mrs Black would hoard medicine meant for keeping sick old people alive and then sell it back to clinics through her phoney drug company – as easy as collecting money every time you pass GO! But some old folk actually died! And as for her being a nurse in Africa and all that . . . *LIES!* Or, as Violet Rose would say, *'pork pies'*. Except, the scar . . . that's dead true. She has one . . . slashed across her left cheek. But *that* she got as a kid in a street fight with the Northside Chuggy Chicks. Lastly, the only thing Mrs Black *ever* got from Her Majesty was four stiff prison sentences – five, counting the one she's serving right now.

When the judge heard how his mother had bullied and beat him since he was a child, making him steal and lie, Blaire got off lightly. Mind you, it helped that he led the police to his aunt Brenda's flat in Bromley where all the loot was stashed, including a safe stuffed with jewellery and bank notes.

So in the end, Violet Rose got back her stolen money, and the Major his oil painting, and we were very happy about that.

Now, I suppose this is a bit of good news – for Blaire, anyhow.

Instead of sitting in jail, he has to attend therapy sessions for *deeeeeeply* disturbed hairdressers and do community service. Lucky for him, the old ladies at Lady Buxom said he could return and do their hair and nails because he's so good at it – but he's not allowed to charge! Sophie's very happy about him getting a second chance. In fact, being Sophie, she thinks the Horned Heart should also be let off. 'She probably had a wicked granny who was mean to her when *she* was a child. And that's why she hates old people,' she tries to convince me. *Doh!*

*But here's the BIG news:*

We had our photo taken with Violet Rose for the *Village News* and some antique-jewellery-expert-bloke saw the brooch she was wearing and recognized it as a genuine *Louie-something-or-the-other love brooch* . . . worth a fortune!

Immediately, Violet Rose flogged it and got her eyes fixed . . . some other things as well, I think, because when we last saw her she was looking quite a bit like a *Coo Ca Choo Girl* again.

'S'trewth, duckies!' she told us. 'When they done me eyes, I could see *clearly* that I needed a whole lot more renovating done, didn't I?'

Gran says she went a bit wild, buying her friends things they've always wanted. Mr Broomhall got an iPod so Julian could download lots of music, including the new CD by *The Test Icicles*.

Miss Avery got a furry purple seat cover for her potty-chair, and a kitty-cat toilet-roll holder.

The Major got a major hair transplant . . .

. . . and Sailor Flynn now has a tattoo of Puffin Muffin – all the way from his neck down to his belly button!

The rest of the residents got a year's supply of *BioBooster Multivitamins for Seniors.* 'The place is buzzing!' says Gran.

Violet Rose had plenty left over to get new things for her room.

So she gave Sophie her peacock feather and what was left in the bottle of her *Midnight in Paris* perfume.

Julian got an old bedside alarm clock, which he's going to take apart. He says it might have some first-generation digital technology for his old-tech collection.

And me?

Well, I didn't end up inheriting some old biddy's fortune, but I *did* get a castle – as predicted by the Great Raymoondo.

Only, it's in a frame!

# Chapter Eighteen

'Turn it down, Androids!' hollers Mr Maythem.

We're back at school and he's given us five minutes *max* to talk about our holiday community service projects. There are lots of interesting reports. Everyone says they've learnt stacks by getting involved with their communities.

'I think I'd like to work with animals when I leave school,' says Gabby Bernstein.

'I appreciate what I have a *lot* more, after seeing how the homeless live,' says Paul Trotter.

'We were given gloves, so cleaning the canal wasn't as gross as we thought it would be,' says Stephen Riley.

'Now all you need is a bath!' shouts out Taj Naidoo, and we all laugh and go – *'Pooo!'*

Then it's our turn.

Sophie talks about working in the hair salon with old folk, and how much happier they felt after having their hair done.

Julian's very funny about Mr Broomhall and his computer. 'The first time I met Mr Broomhall,' he tells the class, 'he was holding his mouse up to his computer screen, clicking it like a remote control.' The class fall about laughing. 'But,' says Julian, getting serious, 'it's medically proven that old people live longer, healthier lives if they keep their brains active. And you can't fall asleep on *Roadkill*!'

That leaves me. And I go for all the juicy bits.

I describe in *full* detail the evil Mrs Black and her potty-mouth – calling old people horrid names and all. They cheer at the part when she gets vomited on. They roll on the floor at my demonstration of the Puffin Muffin dance. And they're pretty freaked out by Raymoondo's predictions and how they came true. I'm way over my five-minute slot but I've captured everyone's attention and I'm totally lost in my own adventure. I'm funny that way – like a storybook bursting out of its own cover!

'You should have seen my gran! Using her mystical Yubiwaza skills and her supernatural balancing abilities she paralyzed the most wanted criminal in Britain with just *one* finger!'

Afterwards, Sophie says to me, 'Golly, you made all of that up about your gran, didn't you?'

'No, no I swear, it's true,' I say, '*every* word of it! Gran may *look* like your regular gran but she's *lethal*! If she didn't love teaching art to old folk so much, she could *easily* be in a super elite crime-busting unit and take on a *pack* of Mrs Blacks . . . *and* still be left standing on her platforms. *Swear!* You don't mess with my gran . . .'

By the way, the *second* most funny thing about me is that once I'm on a roll there's absolutely *noooo* chance . . . *none* . . . *whatsoever . . . of stopping me . . .*

Wayne Skinner
← World's Über Wedgie Champ

Not if you plugged my nose with sausage rolls, and *then* gave me an über wedgie

Not if I was pinned down and *every* member of *The Test Icicles* threw up all over me, *after* noshing on *extra-large* Bombay Pizzas at Raymoondo Banergee's Curry Café

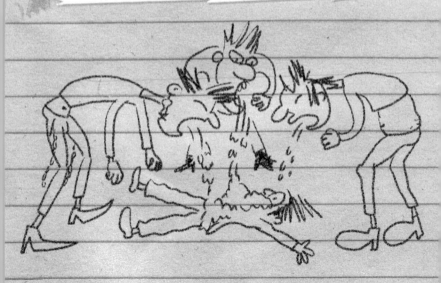

Not even if, *after* being vomited on I was dumped into a fly-infested sewer . . .

of ever...

ever...

# Stopping me!

Now . . . have I told you about the time . . .

**Read on for the exclusive first chapter
of Al's first adventure,
*Operation Itchy Bum*.**

# Chapter One

If I had any say in the matter, I'd be called James … James Bond, even Bernie Bond. But as it happens, my name's Alistair. You can call me Al – Dad does. Mum says there's no sense wasting a good name, so she calls me Alistair, and sometimes 'Alistair D'Arcy McDermott' when she's got something important to say to me, like –

'Alistair D'Arcy McDermott, your dad and I have decided to call it a day and go our separate ways. You're coming with me.'

That was a year ago – one lousy year ago when my dad and mum separated.

'Bye, Al my Pal,' I hear Dad say. 'And remember, it's not your fault that your mother and I are splitting up. It's just that there are times when grown-ups need to go their separate ways.'

Whew! There I was thinking that I had driven him away by:

Painting Mr Smiley on his laptop screen when I turned five.

Playing with the handbrake in the Lake District when I turned seven.

Failing my annual eye test when I turned nine.

... and worst of all,

The time I faked my first tomato sauce death scene in the shower.

There were others,
but that one was the best.

Mum and I live in a block of flats called
La Range. It should be called De
Ranged because the toilet flush
causes the water pipes to
rattle, which causes Mrs
Newhardt's cat to leap two
floors on to Phelps, the
gardener, who sprays into
Creepy Mr Freedlander's

apartment, causing Creepy Mr Freedlander to use language that Mum says is not fit for my ears. Hah!

After they split up, Dad got himself a one-bedroom flat with a 'C' view. He looks straight into the second 'C' of a giant Coca-Cola sign.

At night it makes the flat glow like a night club. It's cool … in a grotty way.

Another cool thing about spending weekends with my dad is his cooking. He's the world's worst cook. So we eat stacks of takeaways. Dad read an article that claims there's no such thing as 'junk food'. Only food that tastes like junk – the kind he cooks. So he doesn't.

My dad's a bit of a brilliant slob. The kind of guy who farts about in his pyjamas (I mean, literally major butt-burpers!) over weekends, while reading technical books, making sketches and writing notes. Mum says he's a bit of a Leonardo da Vinci – all work, no play. Mum's different. She loves going out and having a good time. Dad says she a 'people's person'. Maybe that's why they split up. Dad's not a 'people', he's a person – a nice, odd sort of nerdy man person.

A lot of my friends' parents are divorced. Some of them sound mental. Like a boy in my class, Neal Downe. I swear, that's his name! Well, when Neal's dad fetches him for a weekend, he's not allowed in Neal's mum's house. He has to stand on the doorstep. It can be hailing golf balls and the poor dude has to stand outside. Sophie Ross's mum won't even let her dad see her because he has a young girlfriend who's a real babe. My mum and dad aren't like that. I mean, just because you don't love someone any more doesn't mean that you HATE them, right?

'Your mother loves you more than anything else in the world,' my dad always tells me.

'There's not a thing your father wouldn't do for you,' is what my mum always says.

That's cool. But the best thing they could *both* do for me is to pause … rewind … and start all over again.

'Wake up and smell the poo, Al!' is what my best friend, Sophie, always tells me when I mention 'the separation'. I think she means 'coffee' – which means I should get real. Well, there's something I want to tell you. I don't give up that easily … as you'll soon see!

## Meet Dave. He's disgusting.

At least, that's what his older sister thinks. But Dave knows better: he just wants to know how things work. Even things like burping and farting.

Join him in the lab and you're sure to be grossed out!

www.hodderchildrens.co.uk

Hodder Children's Books